I0459858

EXTINCTION

PHILLIP TOMASSO

EXTINCTION

Copyright © 2015 by Phillip Tomasso
Copyright © 2015 by Severed Press

www.severedpress.com

All rights reserved. No part of this book may be
reproduced or transmitted in any form or by any
electronic or mechanical means, including
photocopying, recording or by any information and
retrieval system, without the written permission of
the publisher and author, except where permitted by
law.
This novel is a work of fiction. Names,
characters, places and incidents are the product of
the author's imagination, or are used fictitiously.
Any resemblance to actual events, locales or persons,
living or dead, is purely coincidental.

ISBN: 978-1-925342-30-7

All rights reserved.

This one is for my daughter Raeleigh.
The story was all her idea.
I just put it into words.
And yes, my Princess, if I make millions you will get
your piece of the pie.

CHAPTER 1

Braddox Founding piloted *Liberation*. Once out of *Clandestine's* bay, he engaged thrusters. The bridge was soundproof, only slightly larger than the cockpit of a fighter ship, and prevented him from hearing the rockets flare. He knew well enough what thrusters sounded like having worked on ships back home. There was a burst of flame from back engines and incredible heat. The *whoosh* alone could pierce eardrums if protective gear wasn't worn.

The vessel shot forward. G-forces sent small waves of nausea through his stomach. He needed both hands on the controls for the moment; otherwise he might coddle the mild sickness with arms across his gut. Regulators kicked in and balanced the speed with the inside cabin pressure. Soon, it wasn't like they were hurtling through space at all, but standing still. He closed his mouth, swallowed hard, and after shutting his eyes for a moment, the uneasiness settled.

With his eyes once again open, he concentrated on the view from the captain's chair. Beyond the glass was a vastness of black nothing. The universe looked empty except for the few planets and moons visible. And their sun. The star was larger than the one at home. Heavily tinted windows prevented Founding from losing his sight. He didn't stare directly at the fiery ball, but avoiding it took effort. He found his eyes were simply drawn toward it.

Founding never grew tired of missions. Flying through space was an unexplainable high. The Milky Way was four-hundred and ninety light years away from home. He and the crew spent ten years in deep sleep chambers. For a decade *Clandestine* flew on autopilot. Scientists charted the course. Mathematicians made the journey possible. He understood only bare basics. The brains behind the program ensured unobstructed flight paths. Somehow they could calculate and take into consideration comets and known asteroid fields, as well as where planets will be during their orbit around their sun. There were still risks. Assignments like this always came with risks.

The excitement of a new mission is what Founding loved. The risks just made everything much more intense. The thought alone made his blood flow faster. It surged through his veins and arteries at breakneck speed. Blood pressure meds could never manage that kind of stimulant.

In a few hours he'd wake the other three crew members. For the moment, the universe was his. Little steering was required, thanks to top notch engineering, but his being awake first was necessary to provide cursory assistance with having *Clandestine* hold for their return, and preparing *Liberation* for the short journey. This included moving the three sleep pods from the mother ship to this one.

As much as he valued the time alone, the peace, the quiet, the view, what he missed right now was driving tunes. He switched on the preloaded playlist and bellowed like an animal in heat. Uninhibited because there was not a soul awake to complain.

Captain Founding didn't have family at home. None of his crew had families. It was a ten year mission. No one left loved ones that long. Some might, depending on circumstances, but most wouldn't. On a mission that could easily last a quarter of a century, only those with no ties were even considered.

The pool of candidates was picked through with extreme scrutiny. Teams were trained for the exercise and just over ten years ago launched toward planets similar to their own. Overpopulation became an issue. It wasn't surprising. Medical advances prevented unnecessary deaths from disturbing illnesses that plagued the planet since the beginning of time. Their time, anyway. Climate control took away risk of tsunamis and hurricanes, tornadoes and volcanic eruptions. Forest fires during dry seasons extinguished as fast as they began and long before they spread. Droughts and famine were wiped out long ago. The positive aspect of fixing broken things is wonderful. The warned about negative points were realized after it was too late.

The plan in place seemed impossible, but necessary. Scoping out other planets with similar life support properties might be the only way to cure over population. There were other signs of destruction on the horizon as well. Those in charge were tight-lipped about the impending hazards. Founding didn't need a degree in science to predict what was coming. For all of the combined intelligence working toward making the planet perfect, they stifled natural growth and change. No. They barred it from existence. The things done to make everything wonderful were cosmetic, topical. The planet's core was in turmoil. It reminded Founding of when his step-father used to cover his nose and mouth with his big hands. At first it seemed funny. Soon, Founding panicked. His eyes bulged, his lungs burned, and his body reacted to the suffocation. He'd swing his arms and kick and pull away. Eventually, he fought his step-father for survival.

Their home planet was going to self-destruct if it wasn't allowed to breathe.

You can't change what something is. It is that simple. You can't restructure the way something is wired and expect it to work forever. One guarantee that ensured things go from bad to worse was the nearly complete depletion of natural resources. Mining every mineral and fuel source from below every continent and body of water was never a good idea. It became essential to supply the wants and needs, and everyone just figured they'd deal with consequences later. Unfortunately, but expected, it didn't take *later* all that long to catch up.

How did politicians remedy the problem they'd campaigned to create?

There was no winning way to tell everyone you were *now* going to once again allow natural disasters to resume and cured diseases to return. It wasn't even *just* about election victories at that point. Turning tables back to the way things once were lacked any compassion. So rather than fix the entire world, they'd let it implode in silence, wearing phony smiles, convincing themselves nothing was wrong.

If nothing was wrong, then Founding wouldn't be strapped into *Liberation* rocketing toward a blue planet similar to home with expectations of saving his race. It wasn't a secret mission as much as shied away truths about why teams were being sent to investigate nearby galaxies.

Observe. Collect samples. Submit data home.

They were not to interfere.

Twenty-five years on a single mission could mean the difference between having a home worth returning to, or complete extinction.

CHAPTER 2

Aria Light opened her eyes. Through steamed glass she saw a man smiling down at her. He wiped sweat off the encasement between them, and his smile only grew. His dark skin and white teeth seemed familiar. She knew she was lying down, but still felt dizzy, like she might pass out.

The lid over her opened with a hiss-thump. She shook her head as memories filled her brain.

"Wakey, wakey," Captain Braddox Founding said. He held his hands up. "Take a moment before getting up. The system is filling your body with fluids and nutrients right now. You might have a little headache. That's normal. Breathe slowly. Deep breaths. Okay?"

Light nodded. She understood the commands. They'd learned this during training. At first she worried she'd panic. She didn't. She listened to the captain's calming voice. It soothed her.

He continued talking, instructing her to relax, and let the pod wake her insides a little at a time.

Ten years.

She couldn't believe it was possible so much time had lapsed, that she'd slept so long. Most nights she'd been happy to grab four or five hours.

Ten years, though?

It was kind of exciting. "We're on course?"

Founding nodded "Everything looks good. We're on Liberation, and the planet is just over an hour away. We'll be landing soon. When you're ready, fix yourself something to eat, clean up, and meet me on the bridge."

He reached in a hand and helped her sit up. Her head was spinning. She didn't think she'd pass out, though. In a moment her mind and body would settle down. She just hoped she felt rested, because right now she thought she might have to suppress a yawn. "The others?"

"Wanted to see your pretty face before poking Martin awake." He laughed. The deep sound echoed inside the hull of the ship, bouncing off walls. "Doppler should be almost ready."

She couldn't help but smile watching him walk away as he sang some song so obviously out of tune she could not recognize the artist. She rolled her fingers into a fist, and breathed in a deeply through her nostrils, before exhaling in a long, loud sigh. She flexed her shoulder blades, and rotated her head up and down, and from side to side. Bones cracked. It felt wonderfully relieving.

More than food, she wanted a shower. There wasn't water for bathing on *Liberation*. It was more of a chemical spray, a delousing effect.

She didn't care. Her body itched, and getting cleaned off after a decade-long snooze was the only thing she considered a priority at the moment.

Stepping out of the pod, she held onto the side for balance. Her legs wobbled. She let them adjust to holding her weight and studied the surroundings. An array of tubes ran overhead, housing wires and air. Circuit boards were lit with red, green, and yellow lights. Some flickered on and off. Others stayed on. Some remained off. The beeps and chirps meant things were up and running. Always a good thing. The temperature was a little crisp. Dressed only in underclothing, goosebumps were raised on exposed thighs, belly, and arms.

Walking took a little practice. Her toes curled up, and the balls of her feet felt suddenly ticklish with each step she took. The sensation didn't make her want to laugh. She cringed instead and tried setting her feet flat on the cold flooring. Thankful to remove the little clothing worn, Aria stepped under the shower head, pulled the release, and while the thick cloud of chems sprayed her body, she lowered her head and pressed a palm against the tiled wall.

It was over in minutes, and not satisfying at all. Hot water would have been better. She toweled off the residue, ran a brush through her hair, pulled it tight, and tied it off in a ponytail.

Her uniform hung in a locker. She dressed in the tight, black and purple leather jumper, zipped closed from inner thigh to under her chin, and laced and tied up black boots. The belt held a blaster, binocs, and a zip bag of nutrition packets. She checked the look out in the full length mirror. She'd lost not just weight but muscle mass. When there was time, she'd hit the gym. Toning up was important and provided stamina. There was no telling what waited for them on the planet surface. Feeling weak and tired could get her killed and would likely endanger the safety of the other crew members.

With the chem shower out of the way, and fresh clothing on, she was more attuned to grumble and rumble in her belly. The fluids the sleep pod provided might sustain life, but she craved a giant burger, fries, and a milkshake. The four inch energy bar in with her other supplies would have to suffice. The tree bark flavor and cardboard texture left plenty to be desired.

The ship shook. Aria looked up as if she thought pipes had dislodged, or an answer for the turbulent shake came from above. She left the small compartment that was her bedchamber and headed toward the bridge.

Liberation was a fraction of Clandestine's size, but large enough for personal space when she or any of the other three crew members needed time away, alone for reflection, or to preserve one's sanity. She walked the halls toward the front of the ship. They were only as wide as outstretched arms, and the ceiling just high enough she did not need to duck her head. The floors were rubber padded for comfort, but everything else was a depressing gunmetal grey.

The door to the bridge swooshed open.

Captain Braddox was not alone.

"Caldera," Aria said. Martin must have skipped the chem shower. His hair was matted down on one side and flared like ruffled feathers on the other. He was dressed in the black and purple jumper though. She hoped he showered and his hair just looked bad because it was sucky hair that he didn't waste time brushing.

"Light. How was your nap?" Martin grinned. He wasn't a bad guy. Just suffered from a bit of obsessive compulsive disorder. Nothing wrong with that type of personality on this type of mission. You needed people who suffered from tunnel vision. Things only became issues when he couldn't concede to opinions that might actually prove better than his.

"Restless," she said, noticing the contrasting differences between Braddox and Martin. Founding was almost a head taller and more muscular. Martin was thin, thinner than she was. He also had long, bony fingers, and wore black glasses with thick lenses that magnified his eyeballs. "I felt the ship shake. How are we doing?"

"Fine," Martin said. "It was me. Meant to switch off the music, but. . .well, hit a wrong button."

That smile again. She wasn't sure she believed him. It wasn't so much she considered his explanation a lie, as a way of protecting everyone from the truth. Regardless, the captain always seemed happy. She mostly respected such demeanor if it didn't annoy her first thing in the morning when she was at her grouchiest. "Look at that view."

"Third planet from the sun," Caldera said. "The blue one."

She bit back the sarcastic response. "It looks a lot like home. So blue. You know what a good name for it would be? Azure. That's what I would name it. What are there, nine planets going around their star?"

"Eight."

Aria counted them, pointing at them as best she could. "I think I'm seeing nine."

Caldera shook his head. "See that one at the end. Furthest from the center star? That's not a planet."

"Looks like one, to me."

"It's a rock. A big, big rock," he said matter-of-factly. "Definitely not a planet."

"Well. You would know. It looks like it's in an orbit though," she said.

"It's just large enough that it is included in the orbit, but trust me. That is not a planet. I *am* getting pretty excited about landing on— Azure? I like that. Good name," Caldera said. "I can't even imagine what we're going to find. I mean, the place looks like mostly water. Not a bad thing. The clusters of land are huge. If our probes reported correctly, the air is essentially the same. There are trees, and mountains, lakes and rivers. It's an uninhabited paradise."

"Those probes were launched over a century ago," Founding said. "They sent back sketchy images from space and was only able to make calculated guesses around air quality and such. Nothing wrong with feeling excited and getting your hopes up, but we need to be realistic. The chances of the planets being perfect matches is a million to one. A million to one."

Aria heard everything Captain Founding said but shared Caldera's enthusiasm. They were venturing to an unknown planet that allegedly mirrored home. Only the planet wasn't depleted of resources, and as best everyone could tell, there was not one soul.

Aria's heart dropped when the red light on the ceiling in the center of the bridge started spinning three seconds before the alarms shrieked. For a fraction of a second longer, no one moved at all. It was as if the light had hypnotised them.

Paralysed them.

"Braddox?" Caldera said. His tone of voice shot up a few octaves as he bent forward, his legs frozen in place, and reached onto the back headrest of a chair.

Captain Braddox flipped switches. His brow furrowed as he stared at instrument panel after instrument panel. Either he wasn't liking what he saw, or he couldn't find the issue to dislike.

Either way, Aria knew nothing about flying.

"Small asteroid field. Straight ahead. Wasn't plotted by the guru's home," the captain said.

Light didn't see anything. "Can we avoid it?"

"I'm going to maneuver manually. We should be fine. Nothing terribly large on radar. Not that congested. Going around could add days to the trip. We don't have that kind of time or the resources to spare," Braddox said.

"I'm going to check on Doppler!" Aria knew she'd feel better if the co-pilot was in her seat for the asteroid field. It wasn't like they could make an emergency landing and radio home for a tow. Didn't work that way in space.

"Good idea," Founding said. He kept a hand on the control shift between his thighs. "Martin?"

"Yes, sir."

"Why don't you sit down, and strap yourself in," Captain Founding said.

CHAPTER 3

The ship's narrow halls flashed red. The high pitched scream from the alarm shot down every corridor. Aria ran toward Candice Doppler's room. She thumbed the comm link on the shoulder of her suit. "Captain?"

There was a silence.

"Captain?" She tried again.

"Ahh, Aria?" It was Martin. "Ahh, yeah. Captain's pretty busy right now."

She shook her head as she stopped in front of the door to Candice's chamber. "We all know there's an issue. Is there any way to silence the alarm?"

"I think alarms are important," Martin said.

The alarm went off, but not the red lights. Some areas within the hull contained red spinning gumballs like the kind Peacekeepers used on top of cruisers. In other areas, the lights stayed red.

She figured the captain shut the audible. If the blaring whoop whoop annoyed her, it must have gotten under everyone's skin, as well. Maybe not Martin's. That was Martin, though. He needed the alarms; couldn't be an emergency without them.

As Candice's door swooshed open, the ship shook. Aria braced her arms, hands inside the doorjamb. Her legs wobbled. She didn't like this. They were too close to their destination.

Candice was curled up into a ball on the bed.

"Doppler. What are you doing?"

Nothing. No response. Aria walked over and touched Candice on the shoulder. The woman's eyes were open. Her hands were laced together by her face. "What did I do?"

Aria wasn't sure. "What are you talking about?"

"Ten years," Candice said. "We just wasted ten years of our lives. Twenty, really."

"You knew this when you signed up. No one made you go on this mission."

"I just broke up with Kenny. It was over a stupid argument. My fault really. I did this out of spite. Figured I'd show him. You remember Kenny?"

She didn't. It was beside the point. The agency didn't let people sign up for a mission like this, and that was that. There was six months of psychological evaluations. It was a failsafe to prevent exactly this kind of response. "You need to get it together, Doppler. Maybe you didn't hear the alarms, but we've got problems." She stood up and walked back toward the door. "Finish getting dressed. Now. Meet up on the bridge."

Aria stopped at bedchamber entrance. "Let's go, Doppler."

Aria didn't have time or the patience for babysitting. It wasn't what she'd signed up for.

A little hand holding now and then, fine. That she could handle. Candice needed to find her own strength and courage—her own independence. Hand holding wouldn't cut it, and it was far too early in the mission for tears.

Anxious, she nearly ran on her way back to the bridge.

The doors opened. "What's going on?"

"We're through the asteroids. Wasn't that big a field," he said.

"What?" Aria said.

"We did take a hit." Braddox cocked his head to one side as if being slammed by an asteroid was no big deal.

"And?" Aria said.

"And. . .we've got a leak. A small amount of fuel is spilling from one of the tanks." Captain Braddox still sat in the pilot seat, the controls at his fingertips. "It's not a huge leak. Small hole. When we land, we will have to patch it up."

Aria stared at the planet. They were close. So close. It was such a blue world. All of that water was amazing. The images they'd reviewed while home did not do the planet justice. Her imagination ran wild. The alien lifeforms must be spectacular. The idea of discovering brand new species of everything, gathering samples, and conducting research made her heart rate jump. She was surprised the medical staff didn't prescribe high blood pressure meds. Problems with the ship were the last things she wanted to think about. "And the return?"

"Should be okay," he said.

Should be? she thought. "What was with the shaking?"

Braddox tightly pursed his lips. "Not sure. A hiccup. I don't see anything else on the system indicating any other issues. Could just have been the breach to the tank."

"How long until we're down?" Aria tried ignoring the alarms and the bad news. If Braddox wasn't concerned, she wasn't wasting time worrying—or was going to do her best to not worry. If he said he can patch the ship's tank when they landed, then he could. While she explored the surface, he could run diagnostics until he was blue in the face for all she cared. Things she'd only dreamt of doing were close to becoming a reality. There were no new species at home. No new anything. Everything that could be discovered, had been. And used. And was now borderline extinct. Including her race. They had a job. The data collected could be the difference between death and survival. The awesomeness of their responsibility was heavy, and if she dwelled on it too long, crushing. It didn't negate her excitement, but the people on her home planet entrusted the several space missions to find a way to save them. There was no denying that was both heavy and crushing.

"Ten hours. Eleven tops. Where's Candice?" Braddox said, never taking his eyes off the screens. His fingers typed on holo-keyboards. Full color plot points and radar sweeps were three-dimensionally displayed above the dash. With a slide of his hand, they shifted to the far left. He brought up another display. It resembled the solar system they were in. He spread the image, zooming in on their blue planet and the small moon rotating around it.

"Finishing getting ready," Aria said. It wasn't a lie, just not an accurate truth.

Martin sat in the co-pilot seat.

"Don't touch anything," Braddox said.

Martin's hands went up. "I'm not. Not touching anything."

Candice Doppler co-piloted *Liberation*. She was the first one awake after Braddox. She should have been sitting where Martin sat. Instead, she hid inside her bedchamber. That wasn't Aria's business. She and Martin had their work cut out for them when they landed. Martin had a brilliant mind. He just wasn't very graceful. She would feel all around better if he just stood up or sat someplace else.

Candice walked onto the bridge. Talk about timing.

"Sorry I'm late, Captain." She looked well. Her hair was done, uniform on. Aria couldn't even tell the woman had been crying. Had she used kid gloves, who knows what the outcome would have been? Maybe she'd still be fetal and balling like a baby.

"Good morning, sunshine. Kick Martin out of your seat, and we'll run through checks." Braddox Founding tapped at images on his display, expanded known data dumps, read through them, and swiped them away before pulling up additional information.

"Aye, Captain. Martin?" she said.

He stood up. "All yours."

CHAPTER 4

Aria and Martin were strapped into chairs behind Braddox and Candice.

Captain Braddox spun dials and flipped switches, calling out commands.

"Roger," Candice said each time.

They both had throttles in a hand and seemed to steer the ship together.

Watching the exchange was engrossing. Aria admired their skill. She was relieved Candice had managed a one-eighty and was effectively assisting in piloting *Liberation*. It calmed her knowing the assembled team wasn't crumbling before they landed.

The blue planet was so close, had so filled up their view, that Aria was tempted to reach out and see if she could touch it.

White clouds moved in patterns over the planet's surface.

"Looks like a hurricane brewing down the southwest of that peninsula," Martin said. "Hard to tell from here, but looks like a promising storm brewing."

"No fear," Candice said. "We're not landing there. Nowhere near it, actually."

"Looking at the edge of the land mass over there." Braddox Founding pointed.

"Good," Aria said. No storm clouds anywhere near the identified spot. Actual time on the planet was limited. Ten years to get here and ten more to get home, but less than a week on the surface. Almost seemed like a joke. Only there was nothing funny. Had to base the length of stay on supplies. Those at home were anxious for results and data. For them, it felt like they'd just launched. At home, many of the people involved with the mission were likely dead. More would die before they returned. Old age, famine, disease, and plain old accidents would take the lives of most. They'd be welcomed home by people who were in diapers when they left.

"Approaching the planet's atmosphere." Candice Doppler's fingers played over the holo-keyboard, while her eyes scanned the multiple displays in front of her.

"Hang tight. It's going to get bumpy," Braddox said.

Liberation shook. Speed increased. The hull rattled. Aria grabbed onto her seatbelts with both hands. She wanted to shut her eyes but couldn't. If she did, she risked missing something. This entire journey was an adventure. If she didn't go at it with eyes open, what had been the point in volunteering?

"Gravity," Candice said.

"Gravity, check. And drag." Founding kept typing with one hand. His other remained in a tight grip around the throttle.

"Gravity and drag, check," she repeated.

"The gravity alone would make us almost plummet to the planet's surface," Martin said. "The drag is from air particles. It's friction. Creates resistance. Slows us down a little."

"Reaching three thousand degrees," Candice said.

"Shock wave," Braddox said. A fiery plate erupted in front of Liberation's nose. It was force field, and protected the ship from the intense temperatures.

"Well within the atmosphere in three, two, and," Candice said, stopping before she said one.

"Thrusters engaged," Braddox said.

They were no longer at the mercy of gravity or drag. Braddox maneuvered the ship out over a large body of water. They were so close Aria saw the rippling waves in the sea, white caps before the waves rolled onto land.

The beach reminded her of Cladstack Island. It was a place her father took her and her brothers when they were young. They spent long weekends at a cottage on the shore. The days were spent swimming, the nights in front of a campfire. She would never forget roasting food on sticks over the dancing flames. "It's just like home. I don't believe it. It's just like home."

The tall trees were covered in large leaves. The landscape rose. Braddox flew over a mountain range.

"That's where we're landing," Braddox said, pointing.

Aria wanted to remove her seatbelts. She was anxious to explore. "Looks good."

"Glad you approve," Candice said. The bite was in her words. Aria ignored it and instead watched the trees get taller as the ship sank down between them.

"Great landing, Captain," Martin said.

"Why, thank you." Braddox shut down some systems and turned on some others.

Aria unfastened her belts.

"Testing air quality," Candice said.

"And?" Aria said.

"I don't believe this," Candice said.

"What? What don't you believe?" Aria stood over Candice's shoulder.

"Air here is identical to home, except pure."

That wasn't surprising. There was no industry polluting everything. "So we don't need to wear any gear?" Aria hated the idea of space gear. The helmets were bulky and the suits suffocating. She may have passed tests showing she wasn't claustrophobic, but that didn't mean she enjoyed the hot and trapped sensation wearing the suits caused.

"You got to wear them," Candice said. She flung the data from her display over to Braddox with a flick of her wrist.

"It's too pure," the captain said. "Your body won't be able to handle it. Breathe in clean air like that, you risk shocking your lungs. Too much oxygen and not enough pollutants. When we head out we'll be in full gear."

Aria gritted her teeth. She didn't voice her displeasure. She should be thrilled just knowing the air is compatible. That alone made the planet a likely replacement home for her people. With a smile, she could check that off the list of Must Haves. "Aye, captain," she said.

CHAPTER 5

The four of them dressed in grey-white support suits, helping each other ensure everything was correctly in place. The mics were hardwired. They could talk to one another easily.

Braddox said, "When air is low, you'll see a yellow light flash at the bottom of the mask. The helmet will vibrate. It's letting you know—"

"We have twenty minutes of air left," Martin said.

Braddox stared at Caldera. "The helmet will vibrate letting you know you have twenty minutes of air left, max. Could be less. Depends on how fast you're breathing. If you are exerting yourself, it's possible you can use that bit of air up in ten minutes. So be mindful."

Aria nodded. She remembered this from training; they had spent extensive time in suits.

"When you get lower, it will vibrate more frequently. More yellow lights will be displayed. And when you are just about out of air, a red light comes on, and your helmet will vibrate continually. At that point, if you aren't back to the ship, you could be in trouble," Braddox said.

"Before you two go out exploring, give Candice and me a chance to check out the fuel tanks. I want to make sure we're all set here before we head out there," Braddox said.

"Captain," Aria said. She knew her disappointment was expressed in her tone of voice. She didn't care. "Our time is limited. I don't think we should spend too much time on the ship. We need to be out collecting samples."

"Ms. Light, while I respect the work you'll be doing, you need to respect mine. We don't know what's down here. Could be hostiles. If we need to evacuate because you and Mr. Caldera kick up a hornet's nest, don't you think it is important that *Liberation* is in working order?"

"I do, Captain, but—"

"You have a 'but?' Really?" Braddox grunted. "You and Martin can walk around. No further than a hundred yards in any direction. Is that clear?"

"A hundred yards?" Martin said.

Aria quieted Martin with a hand on his forearm. "One hundred yards in any direction. Aye, captain."

Braddox stared at her for a long moment. "We understand each other then?"

"We do," she said.

The captain nodded. "Okay. Then if everyone is ready?"

Martin and Aria picked up small metal cases.

Candice held a tool box. "Ready, captain."

They entered a foyer between *Liberation's* hull and the door to outside.

When the door behind them locked closed the one in front of them opened like a mouth.

The top half of the door rose. The lower have went down, legs extended. It became a ramp.

Aria heard her heart beating in her ears. She could not recall a time she'd ever been this excited. It wasn't about fame. It was about opportunity. They were feet away from stepping onto an alien planet. All the mental preparation was nothing compared to the here and now of the mission.

"Ms. Light?" Braddox said, and waved with his arm like a gentleman.

"You first, captain. You got us here," Aria said. It was difficult being humble. She couldn't deny her feelings. She wanted to go first.

Braddox would be remembered forever as the first man to step foot on the planet's surface.

He deserved the credit.

"Doppler? How about you and I together?"

The suits recorded everything they did, every sound they made. The suits monitored their vitals. Everything could be watched from monitors inside the ship. As the two hooked arm in arm and walked down the ramp, the moment was being preserved forever.

They stepped down and onto soft terrain.

"I feel like we should say something profound," Braddox said. "I don't have anything prepared."

Candice said, "We are quite possibly the first to visit our new next home."

Aria wasn't sure that qualified as profound. It did seem fitting, and the captain seemed to like it.

"One hundred yards," Braddox said. "Check in regularly. And your blasters?"

Aria patted hers. It was in a holster on her hip. "Got it. Set to stun."

"Stun makes sense when we know what we're up against. Right now, we have no clue. Stun might be useless."

"And taking it off stun would be overkill," she said.

"We're not arguing about this. Until Candice and I can explore with you, I want both of you to switch off stun. Understood?"

Wanting to say, *Yes, dad*, Aria simply nodded. "Let's get moving, Martin."

CHAPTER 6

The vegetation was thick. Shoulder-high shrubs with torso sized green leaves grew like groundcover. Trees with brown bark peppered the terrain. Long branches sprouted more but different large, green leaves.

There was no clear path for walking. Martin led the way. His exaggerated steps made sure nothing waited to attack under the foliage.

Aria concentrated on breathing calmly. She listened to the breaths inside her helmet. She wasn't worried about running out of air, not a hundred yards from the ship. She just wanted to preserve as much air as possible so she could spend several hours exploring.

Martin stopped at a small clearing. He shook legs out of the base of his case and opened it up on the makeshift tabletop. The small lab allowed for samples collected to be stored.

Aria set up her case beside Martin's. "I suppose we should start with leaf sections."

They didn't need to discuss a plan. What needed sampling was obvious. They were both experts in their fields. Why she called out the obvious was beyond her. It was a way of getting started, she supposed.

They went to work combing over the area. It wouldn't take long before they'd filled both cases with sections and samples and would need to return to *Liberation* for more empty cases. Gathering a piece of everything was the goal. Doing so would be impossible.

While Aria focused on living specimens, Martin scraped up dirt and rock samples. He bottled air and liquids. He'd run tests back at the lab.

"What's that you have?" she said.

He held a large round object in his hand. It was spherical and as wide as his palm. It had a swirling grey and white and reddish color. "It is some kind of rock," he said, and tapped it with a metal instrument. "It's most peculiar."

She watched him place two inside his bag before she knelt beside the base of a tree. A large insect with a shiny brown and black striped back shell moved over the bark. There were too many moving legs to count. The antenna probed up and down, back and forth. She didn't notice eyes or a mouth. With tongs, she snatched it up and forced the being into a small tube, twisted the cap closed, and dropped it into a bag attached to the belt around her waist.

The smile she wore might be stuck on her face until they returned to the *Clandestine*.

The sun in this system demanded recognition. She knew she sweat inside the suit anyway, but the heat she felt from the rays made it worse. It was like she was being cooked alive. Could that happen? She hoped nights were cooler.

"Aria, are you seeing this?"

Martin loved interrupting her. She didn't call him when she cut a piece of leaf and stored it, or when she saw the bug before she stuck it inside the tube. He'd call her for every little thing. Sure, he was as excited, but who wasn't?

"Martin, I—"

"Aria," he said.

She turned around.

Martin stood by a tree. He held his finger up to his lips. Well, up to the glass around his face, but where his lips would have been. He was telling her to be quiet. He could just have said to be quiet. Nothing outside of the suits could hear him unless he had his speakers on.

Which he wouldn't have on, or shouldn't. There was no need.

She was going to tell him as much when she saw something move.

She stood up slowly.

When the thing moved a second time, she thought her heart might have skipped a beat. Her breath caught in her chest. The animal kind of reminded her of a large bear, but without fuzzy fur. It also resembled a dog, except for its size. There was nothing about the animal that suggested possible domesticated pet. The body was nine feet long from the tip of the nose to the end of a stubby tail and at least four feet tall. Protruding canine teeth were long and sharp. The beast must weigh over three hundred pounds. With short limbs and clawed paws,

Aria did not want to attract unwanted attention. At least she understood now why Martin stopped talking.

When it walked, the muscles throughout its body flexed beneath skin. It moved like a bear. She hoped her suit's camera was capturing everything. The visual documentation would be stunning to watch later. Her mind spun with ideas. As she watched the animal move away from them, she worked out names for the species. She thought, Titan something or other.

She hoped the thing was an herbivore. Something about the teeth told her she was wrong. The expansive chunk of land they landed on suggested if there was one, there was bound to be more. She expected more. It had predator written all over it. What did something like that hunt? Not insects.

"I was able to zoom in on the bear," Martin said. "I think I have some very clear footage."

"The Titanoide," she said.

"The what?"

"I don't know. It's what I am calling it for now," she said. He technically found it first. He might take exception to her naming a species without him. He wasn't arguing, so she left it alone. It wasn't like he wouldn't be allowed to name things. He could, as long as it had to do with dirt and water and rocks. That was only fair.

The Titanoide growled.

Not at them.

She reached for her blaster. She aimed it at the animal.

Martin looked back at her. Saw the weapon drawn, and dropped to his knees. "Are you crazy?"

"I wouldn't hit you," she said.

"You were no marksman in training," he said. "I think we should go back. Wait for Braddox to take us out exploring."

Really? She wanted to tease him. Call his manhood into question or something. There was no point. He didn't seem like the kind of guy to get a joke. If he possessed a sense of humor, he'd kept it well hidden. "We're not going back. Not yet."

"I think we should," he said.

"Then you go back. I've still got over a half of tank of air."

Martin just stared at her. "I think the titan-thing defecated."

"Where?"

"You're the only one I know that could get excited about feces," Martin said. He pointed between the trees. "There. Already has bugs buzzing around it."

She holstered her blaster. Feces. Bugs. How could she hide her smile?

Stepping over the shrubs, Aria cut a path toward where the animal had been. "You see where it went?"

"Once it got past that clearing, it took off into the forest."

"You call that a forest? Looks more like we're on the skirt of a jungle." Aria knelt by the droppings and scooped some into a bag. It sealed. She identified it out loud for an audible record, and then tucked it away in her bag alongside the bug.

"The insects are like flies or mosquitoes, only larger," she said. Martin didn't have to acknowledge. She was talking to him, but again, was also trying to secure an accurate video documentary of her findings. Catching one was not simple. She waited for a few of them to land on the feces. As fast as she could, she scooped them into a bag and sealed it as well.

They'd been on the planet an hour, and she felt the success of the mission in every passing second. Worst thing so far was the need for suits. If they didn't have to wear the suits, the place would be paradise.

CHAPTER 7

Braddox ran a gloved thumb along the side of the gouge in the fuel tank. For steering the ship through an asteroid field, he thought he'd done pretty well. A rock along the tank was unfortunate. The fuel lost made matters worse. He still smiled inside at how well he'd flown. Downright impressive if he did say so himself.

"Looks bad," Candice said. She set the tool box down, and opened it.

"It might be a little worse than I let on, but I don't think we need to panic just yet."

"Lost a lot of fuel. I saw that," she said. "What are you thinking?"

He shrugged, taking a step back and looking at the overall size of the tank. Patching the hole was going to be a job, but doable. "I'm thinking first thing's first."

"Repair the hole," she said.

They worked together. The blue flame from the welding gun affixed pieces of metal over the long hole.

The visors over their helmets protected their eyes.

Candice lowered her welding gun. "Captain?"

He continued welding. They could talk more later. He wanted to finish repairing the tank.

Afterward, they'd have plenty of time for discussing viable options on making it back to *Clandestine*. He wasn't ready to accept defeat. Perhaps he shouldn't have hidden the truth from the others. There was no reason to spoil their work. How effective would their collections be if they thought they might be trapped on the planet? They needed to send data home. That was the mission. Returning was not.

"Captain." Candice Doppler poked him in the arm.

He switched off the welding gun and raised his visor.

Candice held the blaster in her right hand. She was squatting, scanning the dense forest around them. "We're being watched," she said.

He set down the welding gun and removed his blaster from the holster. "What did you see?"

"It was back that way, toward the nose of the ship. I caught it out of the corner of my eye," she said. She rested a palm against the ship for balance. "I don't know what it was. When I looked, it was gone."

"Into the woods?" Braddox said.

"It's what I'm thinking," she said. "What do you think it was?"

He almost laughed. "I didn't see it."

"Right, right," she said.

"Stay calm, Candice. Okay? Calm," he said. "Follow me."

"Whoa, wait. We're going to look for it?"

Braddox held his blaster in both hands. "Whatever it is you saw, I don't want it sneaking up on us while we finish these repairs. We're not going out to look for it. We're just going to make sure it's gone."

She nodded. "Okay. Yeah. That makes sense."

"Just follow me," he said. He walked around her toward the front of *Liberation*. This was another setback. "Light? Caldera? Do you copy?"

"It's Light, Captain. We copy."

"What's your location?"

"About seventy yards north of Liberation, sir," Aria Light said.

"Roger," Captain Founding said.

"What's up, captain?" Light said.

"Just making sure you're following orders," he said. He wasn't sure he sounded convincing. "Find anything interesting?"

"There is life on this planet. Animals."

No kidding, he thought. "Anything dangerous?"

"Didn't seem friendly, captain. But we didn't get close, and we have no intention of engaging," she said.

"Roger." Braddox wondered if he should order them back to the ship. He decided they'd check the immediate perimeter. If he suspected anything. . .what? Out of the ordinary? They were on an alien planet. Everything was out of the ordinary. "New rules, Ms. Light. Seventy-five yards. Not a step further."

There was a moment of silence. He could only picture Light and Caldera discussing an answer, as if they had a choice. He called the shots. They followed the orders.

He could not believe how similar the planet was to home. The colors seemed more vibrant. The greens a deeper green, and the sky bluer. And while the trees looked taller, and the shrubs bushier, he would swear they hadn't left their own solar system. If he hadn't landed the *Liberation* himself, he'd have sworn they merely landed on a remote island at home.

They were several yards beyond the ship.

Braddox knew his breathing had quickened. He didn't want to waste air. His breath fogged the shield. He kept expecting something to jump out of the brush and attack. Candice had his back. He trusted her.

Something broke branches. It almost sounded like an entire tree was knocked over.

"You hear that?" Doppler said. She took a knee. Her blaster was aimed at treetops. "Came from over there."

"Yeah. I heard it." He stared toward where the sound had come from.

Candice had been right. Whatever was beyond the treeline was large. Tall. It was nearly impossible not to think it was vicious.

CHAPTER 8

"There's another one," Aria Light said.

"Could be the same one," Martin said.

Aria shook her head. "It's different. Look at the markings."

She noticed thicker dark stripes on its skin. The other Titanoide wore softer stripes, less pronounced. This was definitely a second animal. There was no need to get closer. She wanted to observe them, though. It was part of their job. Watching the animal behavior would need inclusion in their report. "Let's climb up this tree. We'll be able to watch them safely."

"They can't climb?" He didn't hide the sarcasm.

"They won't see us up there," she said. She didn't know if they could climb. The large claws suggested they might be able to scale a tree. She wasn't sure, though. It seemed safer than following on foot.

Martin said, "Let's head back. We've got some good samples for our first time out."

"Back? We just got out here," she said.

"We don't know what that thing is. I have samples in my case that I am anxious to test. Don't you want to know what type of minerals—"

A long, low growl silenced them.

"Where'd that come from?" Martin said.

Aria spun around. She couldn't pinpoint a location. "It was close."

"Was it your Titan?"

"It could have been. Quick. Get up in the tree," she said.

If they were being stalked, it made sense to hide. The animals might be confused by their scent. If naturally curious they'd be around investigating. Trekking back to the ship could prove dangerous. She reached up and grabbed onto branches. Pulling herself up, she used her toe to get a foothold. Shimmying up a few more feet, she retrieved her binocs, and scanned the area.

"What do you see?" Martin said.

Four of the Titans were together. They had noses to the ground.

"Get up in the tree with me, Martin," she said.

"I think we should head back. Get our cases. We can evaluate the samples we've collected and head back out when Candice and Captain Braddox are ready," Martin said.

She refocused the binocs. The Titans picked up a scent.

It might not be theirs.

They were headed this way.

"Get up in the tree, Martin," she said. "Now."

"They're coming?" His tone of voice faltered.

"Four of them," she said. She stood on the branches, ready to climb higher.

Martin scurried up the bark. His hands locked onto a branch, and he pulled himself up. "Keep going," he said.

She didn't need to be told twice. Climbing higher, she wrapped an arm around a branch to keep from falling. She raised the binocs and looked for the Titans.

They closed in on the tree.

"Shh," she said.

Martin didn't say a word.

They both stopped moving. Their odors betrayed them enough. If they made a sound, the Titans would see them in the tree. If they could climb, then the two of them were as good as trapped.

Martin might have been right. Maybe they should have risked a run for the ship.

Aria wanted to contact Braddox, have him lock in on their position. He'd be able to get them out of this. She just wasn't sure how fast he'd find them. Talking on the radio would give away their location. The Titans were directly below. If these things stood on back legs, they'd almost reach Martin. They hadn't climbed high enough. It was too late to react now.

Martin looked up at her.

Even through their masks she knew he realized the error of where they'd stopped.

His lips moved, as if silently begging her to keep climbing.

She couldn't. He needed to remain silent.

One of the Titan's roared. The others began roaring, too. The beasts low, deep growls vibrated up the branches. Aria felt the sound shake inside her chest.

CHAPTER 9

The Titans stood at the base of the tree.

There was no hiding. They'd been seen. Aria started climbing higher. She knew Martin was right behind her. She moved carefully. A hand on a branch. A foot. Her other hand. The other foot. She didn't want to misstep and risk falling. Each inch higher made her feel safer. She didn't stop and look down. If the Titans were climbing up after them, she didn't want to know.

"Faster," Martin said. "Go, go, go."

She tried. The branches got thinner and more cluttered the higher she climbed.

Eventually, one would snap.

She prepared for it, but hoped it didn't happen. She kept testing each branch with a tug before putting any weight on it.

A yellow light came on inside her helmet, and the helmet vibrated.

Air was getting low.

She knew she was breathing quick, deep breaths.

She wrapped both arms around branches and looked down. The Titans stood with front paws on the trunk. Claws out. The razor-like nails shredded bark off the tree.

The Titans weren't climbing the tree.

"My air's running out," Martin said.

"Mine, too," she said.

The beasts weren't climbing up after them, but they weren't leaving either.

"What do we do?" Martin said.

Aria depressed the button on the comm link. "Braddox! Braddox, are you there?"

Silence.

She waited just a moment, and then tried reaching him again.

"Why isn't he answering?" Martin said.

She didn't know.

# # #

They ran, *fast*, but away from the ship. It was not the best situation. When the giant lizard parted the top of the trees with its head, there was no choice but to run.

The thing chasing them was huge, standing at least thirty feet long, but fifteen feet tall. Hooked talons on its feet dug into the ground giving it traction as it chased them. It made a crying sound, "*Hawwwk.*"

"Keep up," Braddox said.

"Right behind you, Captain," Candice said.

There was nowhere to hide. They cut left and right as they avoided trees, and jumped over and went under fallen branches.

The lizard crashed through them, crushing debris under its feet.

Braddox wanted to stop, drop, turn, and fire. He didn't risk it. He wasn't positive where Candice was, and he wasn't confident a shot from the blaster would do anything. The split second he saw the lizard before taking off, he'd have sworn the scales were hard like a tortoise shell. It might be like plated armor.

They came to a swift moving body of water.

The thing chasing them looked like a lizard. It might be more reptile. Either way, they were out of options. There was nowhere else to go but into the water.

"Jump," Braddox said.

He lept off the bank and splashed into the river. The current was faster than he thought. He couldn't get his footing.

Looking back, he saw Candice doing her best at avoiding the lizard. Its mouth was wide open. Rows of teeth lined the top and bottom jaw. It snapped at Candice's head. Missed.

Her arms and legs flailed as she fell over into the river.

Braddox attempted swimming against the current. It was futile. The suit was being weighed down by the water. He wished he could kick off the boots. There was no way. They were fastened tight, and not meant for easy removal.

The lizard dove head first into the river. That shouldn't have surprised him. Lizards, reptiles, whatever it was, probably thrived in water. He expected the thing to be a fast swimmer, which made his stomach churn.

Braddox said, "It's in the water, Doppler. Swim, Doppler. It's in the water!"

She hadn't popped back up. He wasn't sure if the comms worked. He hoped she could hear him.

He turned and swam with the current. He didn't want to reach the monster any faster than he had to. He imagined its tail swishing back and forth propelling it forward at them like a torpedo.

When he chanced a look back, he saw that Candice surfaced. Her arms waved in the air. Her mouth might have been moving. Nothing transmitted. She might not have depressed the button on her shoulder, or the water short circuited the audio. What she didn't appear to be doing was swimming.

Braddox wished he could still see the ferocious lizard. He hated knowing it was somewhere below them, sneaking up on them.

He knew the attack was coming. Imminent. Not knowing exactly where unnerved him. He kept waiting for the thing to chomp him in half.

"Swim, Candice. Swim!" He couldn't look back. Not anymore. He concentrated on his arm strokes, buried his faceplate in the water, and kicked with his legs. With his eyes open he saw nothing underwater but the air bubbles from his arms swishing through the water. Braddox kept expecting to see the lizard and was thankful every second he did not see it.

He angled left, back toward the bank, swimming toward land. He didn't know where the river led. There could be dangerous rapids or giant waterfalls. Every moment took him further away from the ship.

A low hanging limb was ahead. As he came to it, he reached up. His gloved hands latched on. The branch bent some with his weight and momentum, but luckily didn't snap. He pulled himself along the length of the branch toward the bank. His feet touched the slippery rocks. He thought he'd slip under. He managed to regain his footing. He wouldn't let go of the branch. Walking as best he could, he continued pulling himself closer to land. The mud was a good sign. The water was now only thigh deep, and he was confident he could withstand the current. He didn't underestimate it. One wrong step on a slippery rock, and he'd fall back and be swept away again for sure. He was careful, cautious.

Looking back, he saw Candice. She was following his lead, headed his way. She swam for the branch. Her arms pinwheeled out of the water, cut downward into the water, and came back out, over and over. She was fighting the current as best she could, swimming as fast as possible for safety. He knew she was counting on him to save her.

What she didn't know was that the enormous lizard was right behind her. Despite the beads and streaks down his mask, he saw the spiked spine clear enough. It cut through the top of the water and serpentined toward her, closing the distance far too quickly.

"Come on, Candice!" He removed his blaster from the holster. He fired shots over Candice's head. He didn't think a single shot struck the lizard. If his aim was true, the weapon had no effect on the thing's raised spine. "Come on, swim!"

Braddox wasn't giving up. He made his way back into the water. Not far, but hopefully close enough to extend a saving hand. Candice was moving toward him, fast. He shook his arm at her. "Reach for it, Candice! Reach!"

She might have smiled. He wasn't sure. She used her arms, cutting through the water like a champ. He didn't think she was going to make it. It wasn't fast enough.

The lizard went under water, the spiked spine no longer visible. Maybe a shiny fish caught its attention. He hoped that was the case. Easier prey? A fast meal?

He pulled off his gloves. "You're almost here! Come on, now! Come on!"

She threw an arm up. For just a flash of a second, Braddox didn't think they'd reach. Her hand grabbed onto his wrist. His hand onto hers. He dug his fingernails into her arm. They were too wet, and he worried without a strong hold she'd slip away.

Relieved, he almost laughed at the craziness of the situation. "That was close," he said.

"Too close, captain. Way to close." Her voice was muffled through the mask. He understood her just fine.

The lizard's head sprang up out of the water. The snout was long. Teeth lined both the top and bottom of its mouth. Its scaly flesh was green and red and orange. It sparkled under the daylight rays. Its eyes were beady and locked on both of them.

Braddox drew his blaster. The toe of his boots dug into the mud and he fired off three shots. Aiming was nearly impossible. Should have been simple. It was right in front of him. With Candice on his arm, he was fighting to remain standing against the current. His hip pressed against the creaking branch. It would not hold much longer. He worried it would break, and they'd both plunge back into the river and get pulled once again by the current.

Candice screamed.

The lizard's mouth opened wider. Those rows of teeth dripped water and saliva. Its red tongue vibrated with the sickening sound of its roar. It lunged forward. The current had no adverse effect. It stood against the water as if standing on dry land. The thing must be all muscle.

Braddox yanked on Candice's arm.

The lizard's jaw slammed shut on Candice's leg. She screamed, her eyes wide. Her eyes pleaded with him for help.

He pulled on her arm harder.

It was a tug of war.

The lizard had her leg and wasn't letting go. Candice's blood was swept down the river.

When its teeth chomped clear through her flesh and bone, Braddox yanked again.

He fell backwards, with Candice coming out of the water with him.

The lizard was gone; it had taken her leg as the prize.

Braddox wasn't confident the attack was over. He scurried onto grassy land, dragging an unconscious Candice along with him. Her suit had been compromised. It was no longer protecting her from the elements.

Her leg spurted blood. That was the main concern.

He removed his belt and wrapped it around her thigh. He laced it as tight as possible. He needed to restrict blood flow, or she'd bleed out. He hoped the belt was also tight enough to seal contamination from the breach.

Thunder boomed overhead.

"Candice," he said, gently shaking her by the shoulders. He didn't want her sleeping. He worried she might go into shock. The greater fear he refused to acknowledge. Braddox didn't even want to think about that thing coming back for more.

Something roared.

It wasn't thunder, or it wasn't thunder this time.

Behind them were tall shrubs. He scooped Candice up in his arms and hid them both under large green leaves.

CHAPTER 10

Aria Light was not a trained soldier. She wasn't even military like Braddox and Candice. She had undergone basic boot camp in preparation. It had been a grueling five week program. She was in the best shape of her life. The key now was drawing on the skills taught. Survival skills. Combat skills.

They couldn't stay in the tree forever. There had to be a way out of this mess. Getting back to the ship was the only option. Trusting the others could handle themselves, she leveled her blaster as best she could, closing one eye, and targeting the head of a Titan. "Move to your left, Martin," she said.

He threw an arm over his head. "Don't shoot me!"

"It's why I told you to move," she said. She opened both eyes. Doing so made her see double. The barrel was lined up with the Titan's skull though. "Move!"

Martin shimmed to his left. "That's the second time today you tried to shoot me!"

His movement stirred up the animals below.

"It's the second time today you've been in my way!" she said.

Her target was out of the crosshairs. She fired, regardless.

She saw blood before she noticed the exploded head. The Titan dropped. She heard its body crash on the ground. The other animals growled, and roared. They clawed at the bark, desperate to climb the tree.

The one now on top made progress. With claws dug deep into the tree it pulled itself upward. As it removed a front paw, though, it fell. Claws plucked from it stayed wedged into the wood.

The Titan howled, clearly in pain.

Aria fired again. She wasn't sure how many shots the blaster held. Wanting to conserve ammo, she didn't shoot blindly, but tried to line up each blast.

She missed, though.

There were only two left.

They took turns jumping up at them. They each got close to Martin's feet. He shrieked each time as if his foot had been chewed off. She wanted him to shut up. His crying wasn't doing a thing to help the situation. If anything, it added to the tension. "Stop it!"

"They're going to get me!"

Aria ignored him. She lined up another blast.

Before she could pull the trigger, trees fell over.

Martin even stopped whining.

The Titans refocused their attention.

The beast coming at them was over forty feet long. It's swishing tail toppled trees in its wake. The snout extended out six feet and was filled with teeth. A spiked spine started mid-neck, rose along the back, and then descended before the tail. It was bowed, sharp, and appeared to grow out of the vertebra. Aria was both horrified and intrigued.

Before she could bask in the revelation of recent discoveries, the giant creature snapped its jaws closed over the head of a Titan. It rose in the air, standing erect. The body of the Titan flailed inside the jaws, hind legs kicking out.

The remaining Titan didn't take the opportunity to flee. Instead it lept into the air and latched claws and teeth onto the spine lizard's neck.

The spine lizard had small front. . .arms. They almost seemed useless. The lizard attempted grabbing onto the Titan tearing at its flesh.

Martin whimpered.

Aria kicked the top of his head. "Shh!"

When the spined lizard was done eating the Titan, she hoped it would be full and go away. If it wanted, it could pick them out of the tree easily.

Too easily.

Martin was looking up at her. She pointed toward the treetop. They needed to get higher.

Her mask vibrated. Yellow lights flashed inside the mask.

She climbed slowly, carefully. The spined lizard was preoccupied. It might not notice their ascent.

There was the sickening sound of crunching bones.

She stopped and stared.

The spined lizard dropped the Titan out of its elongated jaws. Its headless body crashed onto the one she'd shot with the blaster.

The second Titan continued its attack. Viciously its claws dug into the spined lizard's neck. Blood spilled from the gouges. The Titan's teeth pierced the scaly skin and pulled away chunks of meat.

The spined lizard let out something like a scream; the sound was high pitched, shrill, and alarming. It made Aria want to let go of the branches and cover her ears.

The spined lizard ran. It pushed through trees, missing the one they were hiding in. The tail swung wildly, and it slammed against the base of the tree. The sensation rocked the trunk. Wood splintered.

When the spined lizard was almost gone, Aria saw their chance.

"Climb down," she said. She knew she was yelling.

"Are you crazy," Martin said.

"Go, go. Down! This is our best chance!" She stepped down a branch, but Martin blocked her way. "Move it!"

"We're going to get killed."

"We can't stay up here! Those things will be back."

"I can't," he said.

"We need to get back to the ship!"

Her mask vibrated. The flashing yellow lights returned. "We're almost out of air. If we don't make it back to the ship now, we're dead either way!"

CHAPTER 11

Peering out between leaves, Braddox Founding wondered where all the monsters went. Candice was in bad shape, and she'd lost a lot of blood. The medical back was on the ship; even with it, he wasn't sure how much could be done to save her life. There was no way he'd leave her body on this forsaken planet. They couldn't remain hidden much longer, but wasn't sure how much sunlight remained. He feared once night arrived, more beasts would come out of the jungle, hungry and ready for stalking prey. Especially wounded prey.

No. It was time to move; time to act, not react.

He stood up, Candice in his arms. She was a solid woman, muscle was heavier than fat. He wished she didn't spend so much time working out. Carrying her was not going to be simple. Cradling her in his arms like a child wouldn't work. He wanted his blaster drawn, and ready to fire.

Slinging her over his shoulder, he positioned her body as best he could.

She moaned.

That was a good sign, just bad timing. "I've got you," he said. "Be still. It's going to be okay."

There was no response. She wasn't alert, and he knew she was at risk for going into shock. He needed blankets to keep her warm.

As he stepped out of the brush, he thought about her leg. The open wound was a danger. She was exposed to alien elements. He worried about infection. He had to cauterize the stump. That would take care of the bleeding.

The jungle was thick. The trees tall. The forest floor riddled with vines and fallen branches. He didn't think about the creatures underfoot he couldn't see. He heard them though. They scurried away, mostly. Perhaps they considered him a threat, a larger predator. That was fine. He wanted it that way. There'd been enough confrontation already.

Running would have been ideal. It just wasn't possible. Sweat dripped from his hairline, it ran into his eyes. The salt burned. He gave up trying to wipe away the beads. He pushed through the discomfort.

Every time a branch snapped under his weight, he cringed. The sound seemed to echo around him. At first he'd stop and listen. If anything was following him, stalking them, he was making their task easier. Eventually he gave up on listening. It didn't matter.

He was dangerously low on air.

The hum inside his helmet was constant. The yellow warning lights were at the end. Soon red lights would display, and he'd be out of air.

He couldn't regulate his breathing, not with Candice on his shoulder. The combined weight, and heat, and fear—he knew he was breathing too hard, too fast. He wasn't lost, but wasn't sure how far away they were from the ship. The river had carried them quite a distance. He knew he needed to head north and eventually east. Although everything looked the same, he was confident he'd recognize areas he'd passed. While running. While being chased by a giant lizard.

The mission wasn't a failure. One lizard didn't cancel out a chance for immigration. The lizard was an issue, but back home they had animals that were deadly. They also studied those animals and put many of them in zoos for the population to visit and gawk at. It was how things were done.

He knew, though, that doing the same thing here that was done back home would end with similar results. Something needed to change.

The concept of change was beyond his pay grade. He was one person.

A pilot.

He had his mission, and nothing else.

Part of that mission was getting everyone safely to this planet, and more importantly, getting them all back home. Alive.

He hoped the crews en route to scope out other planets were going better.

There was a small clearing ahead. He could see it through low hanging leaves. The small stretch of field looked familiar.

When he reached the edge of the trees, he stopped. He rested his shoulder against the tree, and finally wiped away sweat.

He blinked twice, just to ensure he wasn't hallucinating.

Not forty yards away was *Liberation*.

People were blessed with different talents. Braddox loved his awesome sense of direction. It was a little thing, but when needed, like now, it came in handy.

He scanned the clearing. There were no visible lizards. It didn't mean the coast was clear, it meant he couldn't see an immediate threat. Big difference.

Raising his blaster, he stepped away from the tree, and using what he had left, he ran.

Candice's body bounced on his shoulder.

His one arm was wrapped around the back of her legs. He didn't want to drop her. There was no way he would slow down or stop until he reached the ship.

He was halfway there when another lizard crashed through the trees on his right.

The lizard was twice as large as the one they'd already been attacked by.

This one had a bowed spine that fanned across its back. The long tail wagged left and right, knocking down trees around it. Its feet pounded the ground, and the ground actually shook. The reverberation from its weight as it ran felt like tremors, as if the ground were about to crack open and swallow them down to the planet's core.

CHAPTER 12

Out of the tree, Aria spun around. "Which way to the ship?"

Martin shifted his bag full of rocks from one shoulder to the other. "I'm not sure."

They were lost. If they started in the wrong direction, they'd waste time and air. They couldn't stand there confused. Waiting for Martin to decide was pointless. He was all scientist and little help outside of textbook smarts. Problem was, right now she didn't trust herself. The spined lizard had destroyed so much of the jungle nothing looked familiar.

"I think we came from over there, that way." Martin pointed.

He was trying.

He was also wrong. "That doesn't look right," she said.

They were killing too much time with indecision.

"Fine. Let's try it," she said. "Where's your blaster?"

"I didn't bring one," he said, and pursed his lips.

She hadn't been excited about wearing a weapon. She was a scientist. Understanding they were in a foreign world helped her decide though. She was thankful she had the blaster. "Stay close. Keep quiet. We don't want to draw any attention."

Both masks began shuttering.

Martin looked like he was being eaten alive. His hands went to his face, and he took several steps backwards. He stumbled over a log and fell. His hands flew behind him, breaking the fall.

Aria breathed in three breaths. The mask was now being sucked in against her face. The air was gone.

She realized her hands were at her face, too.

They were going to suffocate.

Her fingers tentatively touched the corners of the facemask.

There was no more air.

She was sucking on nothing.

Her fingertips unfastened the helmet.

Martin reached an arm out toward her as if warning her to stop.

There was no stopping. They would die with the masks on. The air on the planet was similar to home, just too clean. The irony. She'd trusted her lungs were blackened enough, hardened enough, they could handle some clean air.

She pulled off her mask, and inhaled a deep breath.

Holding it, she waited for a moment. There was no telling what would happen next. Part of her expected a burning sensation in her chest, unbearable heat growing more intense until her lungs imploded.

It didn't happen.

Martin rolled onto all fours, ripping his mask off his face.

He was gasping, coughing, sucking in breath after breath of alien air.

She exhaled and then sampled another deep breath.

Her lungs weren't on fire. She wasn't suffocating. Her body wasn't shutting down. The air might be clean, and alien, but it worked. She was alive. Living. Breathing.

She knelt next beside Martin and placed a hand on his back. "Slow down, Martin. Slow down. Breathe slowly. In. Out. In. Out."

She inhaled through her nostrils. Exhaled out of her mouth.

It seemed impossible, but she tasted the difference. Smelled the difference. She could not believe how pure she felt.

Her grandfather told stories about camping in the wilderness. He'd load up the family and a tent. They would drive out of the city, leaving smog and crime and technology behind. For a week they lived in the mountains and fed off the land. They fished and hunted for food. At night they sat around a campfire; the sky was lit with stars. Those same stars were in the sky when home, but city lights dimmed the view to almost non-existent.

By the time her father was in school, though, most of the forests were gone. The mountains were littered with dwelling complexes. The space was too valuable.

She remembered always wanting a vacation like that, and her father always saying he wished he could take her, that the experience was like nothing else he could compare it to.

Here she was on an alien planet, and except for carnivorous giant lizards, she couldn't help imagining this was as close as she'd come to vacationing in the mountains with family—if the mountains were replaced with a dangerous jungle, and Martin was substituted for family.

She wanted to laugh, but refrained. "Martin?"

He finally stopped gasping. Still coughing, he sat up on his heels. He clapped a hand against his chest. He took slow, deep breaths. His eyes were wide. They stared at Aria in disbelief. "We're breathing."

When he smiled, she smiled back. "This is good. We're good. Now we just need to find the ship."

"We're okay. We're going to make it," he said.

She wouldn't deny him hope. They were far from safe, lost in a jungle of predators. If he needed a crutch, she'd let him have it, especially if it helped him run faster. "We're going to make it!"

Several yards away, the ground cover began parting.

Twigs snapped.

Aria saw something jump and then disappear.

Whatever was running at them was small, low to the ground.

There was more than one.

"Martin," she said, standing up and grabbing him by the arm. "We have to go. Now."

Martin looked back. He must have seen what she saw. He let Aria help him to his feet. They didn't discuss which way to go next. They just ran.

The things behind them closed the gap quickly.

Aria kept looking back, firing blindly, and hoping she either hit something, or the sound of the blast would scare the creatures away. Nothing screamed in pain. And from what she saw when chancing a peek, more of those things—whatever they were—had joined in on the chase.

Martin was several feet ahead of her. She wouldn't have thought he could run so fast. Firing off useless shots slowed her down. The things closed the gap between them. The way they lept over the logs and fallen branches, they'd be on her in seconds. She pumped her legs as hard as she could. She watched the ground. If she tripped and fell, it was over.

The things were squealing. Squeaking. Either they'd just started making the noises, or they were so close she could hear it now. It wasn't good. It meant they were excited. They knew they'd catch her.

She couldn't outrun them.

There was no way she'd give up.

She had to make it back to the ship. Their world depended on the samples collected. They needed to know about the creatures roaming the planet.

She wanted to make it back home.

Squal. Squeak.

They were closer.

Close.

She ran faster, as fast as she could.

Her lungs now felt like they were on fire. It wasn't the air she breathed; it was the cardio she wasn't ready for. All of her training, even in boot camp, hadn't prepared her for this type of chase.

She kept seeing herself tripping.

Grace was never her strong point.

Shrieking came from above—an ear piercing sound. It made her bones shake. Shielding her eyes from the sun, she looked up.

Three giant birds flew through the air. The wingspan had to be over fifteen feet wide. The body was long, thin. They had tails.

As if communicating with their shrieks, they dipped down and dove right at her. She crossed her arms over her head for protection from sharp talons on the end of three-toed feet.

The toe of her boot caught under something. She was flung forward. She landed on outstretched hands.

She rolled over onto her back, ready to face death.

CHAPTER 13

There was little time for thinking. The lizard with the bowed, sharp spine ran at them. Braddox placed Candice down in the tall grass. It was his only option. Otherwise, they'd both die.

"Don't move," he told her. "Stay still! You hear me?"

He stood up.

"Stay still!"

As he ran, waving his arms, trying to draw the lizard's attention, he yelled, "Don't move!"

He ran to the west, away from the river, away from the ship, away from Candice. "Here I am! Come get me! Hey, come and get me!"

He hoped the thing changed course and was chasing him now. He wanted it to leave Candice alone. He didn't look back, but kept waving his arms in the air, and yelling, "Here I am!"

His mask hummed steadily. The lights inside displayed in constant red.

He was out of air.

The thing would have him in seconds. He couldn't get far enough away from Candice to give her a fighting chance.

He breathed hard and fast.

The air was too clean. That was the issue.

There was no other choice. The faceplate was being sucked in tight. There was nothing left to breathe in the tank.

He removed the helmet and threw it aside. He never slowed his pace.

He held his breath while he ran. If he could make it back into the jungle, he could hide, and force the giant lizard to search for his suffocated body. That could buy Candice a minute or two.

She might be out of air as well. Although she hadn't been breathing as heavy. It wasn't like she had been carrying him.

He exhaled. His head felt like it might explode. He didn't want to pass out. He didn't want this thing to catch him.

He breathed in the air as he ran.

The air wasn't stopping him. When he realized he wasn't going to die from what filled his lungs, he felt rejuvenated, almost refreshed. He picked up the pace, and trampled forward back into the jungle. He cut right and left. He lept over logs, and stumps, and anything that might trip him up.

For the first time the thought he might make it, that he could get away from that thing, outrun the giant lizard chasing him.

And then he heard it crashing through the trees behind him.

He only realized other creatures had been chirping and making noises when he couldn't hear them anymore. Everything was replaced by the sound of tall trees falling over. It echoed inside the jungle. The pounding of the lizard's feet sent out ground-shaking tremors. Nothing else under the canopy made a sound. He bet those other creatures were thrilled seeing new prey, him, the attention off them.

I'm losing my mind, he thought.

He would have laughed if he weren't grinding his teeth while he ran. He needed a place to hide. If he couldn't find somewhere soon, the monstrosity would catch and eat him.

Of all the things he worried about prior to the journey—never waking up from the sleep chamber, flying way off course, asteroids blowing up the mother ship—he never once feared he might get eaten. It had never crossed his mind. Maybe he expected semi-intelligent alien life forms, but nothing like this. Not in his wildest dreams. Lizards as tall as buildings chasing him through a jungle had never been on his radar.

He hoped his running helped Candice. She had mostly been out of it when he set her down. She'd lost so much blood, he couldn't expect much from her. She might not have the strength to get to safety, to get back to the ship.

Seeing two completely different lizards forced him to accept truths. There had to be more out there. Maybe a variety of types, species. It only made sense. These lizards were the alphas on the planet. Nothing else stood a chance against them. He couldn't imagine a colony from home settling down here. The blue waters and the vegetation all looked good. The air was more than breathable, and it was preferable. He noticed the difference breathing it in and out. It tasted and smelled clean. There wasn't smog and stench associated with it like back home.

They couldn't survive.

The giant lizards would decimate a colony.

Even a heavily armed colony.

Blasters didn't seem to affect the lizards at all. Their scales, or shells, or whatever it was that made up their. . .skin, was like armor. Impenetrable armor.

There was only one viable option. He was small, compared to the thing chasing him, and low to the ground. He could hurdle debris, cut left and right easier. Best chance at surviving was if he kept running. Stamina.

The fresh air felt amazing inside his lungs.

He watched his footing. Every step he made could be his last. There were too many obstacles. He set palms down on a log, threw his legs over, and continued forward. He dodged thorned branches.

Without looking back, he knew he was putting distance between them.

It was slowing down.

He wasn't sure how far they'd run from the ship. There was no way he was confident they'd gone far enough.

Whistling while he ran and waving his arms, he opened antagonizing the lizard worked. If that thing gave up on him, it might turn back and hunt down Candice.

That wasn't acceptable.

He couldn't hear trees falling.

How long had it been since he'd heard wood splintering?

Looking over his shoulder, he came to a stop.

The lizard was no longer behind him. . .

He heard someone screaming. He didn't think it was Candice, though. It had to be someone else.

CHAPTER 14

Aria couldn't believe she was about to die. This journey was supposed to change her life. She didn't care about fame. She didn't volunteer for the mission so when she returned home she'd be in demand. It wasn't ever about the interviews, the celebrity-status associated with her name, with her accomplishments, and with the research conducted, or because she'd helped find a comparable planet worthy of colonization.

If she received any popularity, so be it. She thought about some of these things, of course. And before they'd launched, she'd been on late night talk shows and morning TV. It was exciting and a bit surreal. It didn't matter, though. It was just heightened daydreaming.

What she wanted, hoped for, was far more basic, and something she'd always felt denied. Above all else, she wished for love and marriage. She wanted kids.

Her days were too routine. She went to work, home, to bed, and repeated the cycle six days a week. Although she would never give up her career, she wanted to share her life with someone. She longed for a family.

Now she knew she had been dreaming.

It would never happen. Couldn't. Dead had a way of preventing the future.

The things coming at her resembled rats, but were the size of dogs. They looked hungry. Big round black eyes locked on her. There were no whites. No pupils. The entire eyeball was black. Immense fangs lined the mouth under twitching white whiskers that looked more like sharp, dangerous quills.

Some of the monstrous rodents hopped over everything in the tall grass. Others charged forward, leaving a path of trampled blades behind. They were all headed directly for her. The end had come. She saw no way out of this.

The giant birds in the sky reminded Aria of bats the size of albatross. The wingspans gave the impression of space fighters from back home. If lasers beams shot from the bird beaks, she wouldn't be surprised. Nothing about this planet surprised her anymore. A beautiful world with plenty of water, trees, and a variety of terrain seemed like an answer to their wants and needs. The deadly lizards brought an element no one expected. She only hoped the other recon missions had better luck; were safe on the planets they ventured toward. One of the teams had to find a new home, or everyone on her planet was doomed.

Aria's breath caught in her lungs as a series of unexpected things all happened at once.

As she was about to turn, a last ditch effort at fleeing, a huge rat leapt onto the small log she'd tripped over and then launched itself in the air toward her. A massive bird dove from the sky. Talons clutched the rat and swooped away.

While she thought nothing about the planet could surprise her, it was Martin who ended up stunning her most. He jumped in front of her, her blaster in *his* hands. He screamed as he fired. His shots hit nothing. He kept shooting, kept yelling. He panned left and right. The blaster spat rounds in a constant, *chig-chig-chig-chig-chig*. Flames shot from the mouth of the barrel.

One rat exploded. Then another. A third's head splattered the fourth behind it.

A fifth jumped toward his chest.

His scream went from adrenaline-wild to terrified as the octaves rose, crackling in his throat. He dropped the blaster as the rat latched onto him. His hands went to the rat's neck in an attempt to keep from being bitten. The weight of the rat knocked him backward. Its hind legs dug fast and furious threw his suit and into his flesh.

He lost his balance, and fell backward, but before he hit the ground, a second bird stabbed six sharp talons from its two claws into his body. Two pierced just under the front of his collarbone, four were thrusted into his back. With a flapping of wings that sounded like a hurricane unleashed around her, Aria watched the bird lift Martin and the flailing rat into the air.

She rolled over in the grass and retrieved the dropped blaster. On her knees, she aimed as best she could before firing. If she couldn't bring down the bird, hitting Martin might not be horrible. His screams echoed down from the sky.

The bird's head raised up. One claw released Martin.

Aria fired on the creature again.

The rodent caught fire and fell away. It hit the grassy ground and scurried off toward the trees; if she didn't know any better, it cried the entire way.

Holding the blaster up and out, she closed an eye and trained the crosshairs on the bird's underside, aiming right for the gut. She squeezed the trigger over and over. The recoil from firing the weapon slammed repeatedly into her shoulder. She didn't stop until the thing squawked, faltered in its flight, and finally released Martin.

She hadn't killed the bird. It, and the third winged monster, flew away, joining the other that scored a rodent.

Martin hit the ground hard.

He didn't bounce back the way the rat had.

She ran toward him, calling out his name. Her heart was beating wildly inside her chest. He had saved her life.

But for how long?

"Martin?"

She reached him and dropped to her knees beside him. Blood bubbled up out of his mouth. He was alive. His eyes were open. It took a moment for them to find her. His hand rose up. She clasped it into her own. "You saved me, Martin. You saved me."

"My bag," he said. "My bag."

The man was dying, but not selfish. He wanted his samples saved. He proved to be a more courageous than she ever expected. People at home needed to hear about his heroics. "I'm with you," she said, squeezing his hand.

He was looking at her. His eyes didn't seem focused. There was blood behind them. It also dripped from his nose. Knowing she was crying, she tried to hold back her sobs. She wanted her strength showing, her appreciation. "Thank you," she said. It sounded stupid, trivial. She meant it.

"The bag," he said.

His eyes stayed open. Lifeless. She placed her palm on his face and gently closed them.

She looked around. All she wanted was help. There was no one to call on. She didn't want to leave his body here, not in the grass for the animals to pick him apart. The thought made her stomach churn. She heaved and wrapped an arm around her waist.

His bag was slung over a shoulder. She lifted it off him, trying not to stare at his corpse. She hoped his soul was somewhere better. He shouldn't have died like this.

She wasn't going to die like this.

Somewhere behind her a lizard roared.

As much as she didn't want Martin left behind, it was time to go. She needed to get back to the ship. Now.

CHAPTER 15

Aria ran through the grass and back into the thicket of the jungle. She was covered in sweat; the heat was nearly too much. If she didn't know any better, she'd swear her skin was melting off the bone. Banged up and bruised, she held onto her side while she ran. She thought she might have a broken rib from when she fell. She hoped it was pulled muscles, and nothing more. It didn't matter. She couldn't slow down. She ignored the pain and continued on.

To the far right were mountains. Tall red rock formations. There were caves along the cliffside. Holes that led deeper into the mountain. They could actually prove perfect places to hide from giant lizards. She wasn't sure how she'd scale the face, though.

The one thing she knew for sure, *Liberation* was not that way.

She adjusted her course, dismayed by how lost she was. She feared the others were dead as well. She'd been unable to raise any of them on the comm. No one tried to reach her. Racing toward the ship might prove merely consolation, and little else. She was no pilot. No one had ever shown her the first thing about flying. Reaching the ship, alone and the sole survivor would be useless, a mere coffin as her final resting place.

It was something though.

Worst case, she could gather supplies. Food, and weapons, and head for the caves.

The sun was setting.

She noticed the change in the sky. It went from bright, light blue to dark. She wasn't sure how many hours were in a day or in a night. They never explained how fast the planet spun and had only guessed the time it took for the planet to rotate around their star.

She wasn't afraid of the dark.

Spending a night on this planet scared her.

She couldn't even begin to imagine the predators that came out when the dark enveloped the lands.

Parting leaves with both hands, she almost cried.

In front of her, just yards away, sat *Liberation*.

It was right where they'd left it.

They had been so close, if only Martin could have held on a little longer.

Ignoring the fresh tears running down her cheeks, Aria found strength and sprinted for the ship.

She ran without looking back.

She felt certain something was only inches from snatching her up in its jaws.

The memory came back without prompting.

Her father took her water skiing. They were on the ocean, close to shore. The boat had twin engines. She was fourteen and good on the skis. In fisted hands she held the rope tethered to the back of her father's boat. He sped across the ocean, cutting over small waves. She skimmed the surface, hollering for him to go faster, always faster.

She crashed over a wake, tumbled forward, and found herself treading water.

It was a moment before her father realized she'd fallen. He had to turn the boat around and circle back to pull her out of the ocean.

While she waited, she knew—just knew— something sinister swam up from the depths and was moments away from chomping down on her kicking legs. She fully expected she'd be dragged below the surface despite her floatation jacket. Sucking water into her lungs, she'd be drowning at the same time she was devoured.

Only her father reached her, hoisted her up out of the water, and without incident. Every time she fell skiing the same fear returned. Her heart beat so fast. She remembered worrying the creatures below would hear it, be drawn to it, and come for her. They never did. It didn't curb the anxiety.

The same feeling was back.

Stronger.

She was so tempted to look behind her. She knew if she did, she'd trip, fall, and whatever was advancing would catch her.

The ship was right there.

It was within reach.

She knew she was crying, sobbing, as she ran. And against better judgement, she turned.

Nothing.

There was nothing behind her. She almost laughed, full of relief.

She didn't.

Her hands shot out in front of her as she reached *Liberation*. They clapped on steel. She used her shoulder to swipe at tears on her chin as she struggled to open the door.

Was it locked?

She pounded on the door, knowing no one was inside. No one would open it for her.

She was all alone.

A lizard roared. She had no idea where the sound came from. Did her body give off pheromones they smelled? Was her body calling out to them?

She lowered her head against the hull, feeling deflated and defeated.

The ship's door gasped. Slowly, it lowered, opening.

Aria stumbled forward, up the stairs, and into *Liberation*. She was about to yell out hello. There was no need. By the door panel lay Candice. She was missing a leg. "Doppler," she said.

"Outside, grab the torch. It's by the fuel tank," she said.

Aria didn't want to go back out there. Candice must need the tool. There was no way she could deny the request. She tried not to think about it, and just turned around, and went back outside.

It terrified her.

She knew she hadn't been any safer inside the ship, but it had felt that way. It had felt like almost being home.

She stayed close to the hull and saw the area where Candice and Braddox had been working on repairs. She snatched up the welding tool and whatever else she could get her hands on and ran back for the opened door.

Once on the ship, she said, "Close it."

"Where's Caldera?"

Aria shook her head. "He saved my life."

Candice pursed her lips. "We don't have much time. There was a relay transmission from Clandestine. We have to abort the mission."

"Ah, you think?" Aria said. All she wanted was to leave the planet. Azure was nothing like she'd hoped. She set everything down. "Where's the captain?"

"He saved mine," Candice said. She was quiet for a moment. "Okay. Listen, there's a massive meteor shower on the way. Something must have exploded, a moon, a planet, a star, who knows? Debris is headed for this planet. It could prove most devastating." She laughed.

Aria wasn't sure if anything was funny. "Are you okay?"

"We have to stop the bleeding. I need to get us off this planet and back to Clandestine."

"How much time do we have?"

"Hours. Minutes. I'm not sure."

"How do we stop the bleeding?" Aria said.

"You're going to weld the stump," Candice said.

This time Aria laughed. When Candice didn't join in, she stopped. "Wait, you're serious?"

"Dead serious. If I pass out in the captain's chair you'll see the autopilot switch—"

"Autopilot?"

"It will get you right back to the Clandestine," she said, but didn't hold eye contact.

"What else?"

"There's nothing else," Candice said.

Aria didn't want protection. "I need to know the truth."

"The sooner we take off, the better our chances. Depending on the span of that shower, autopilot is not able to maneuver at will. The course back to Clandestine is preset," Candice said.

"So if Liberation's headed right for an asteroid, it won't dodge it?"

"It won't."

"We'd just crash into it?"

"We would."

"And before we do anything, you want me to weld your leg closed."

"It has to be done. I'm losing blood. I could pass out or. . .worse," she said.

Aria bit down on her lip. "I've never done anything like this, like what you want me to do to your leg."

"Grab the welder. I'll give you a quick lesson," she said.

Something banged into the ship's hull. Aria screamed!

CHAPTER 16

The bang came again.

And again.

Aria stared at Candice. "It's knocking."

"Open the door," Candice said. She lifted the blaster next to her.

Aria reached over Candice's head. She depressed the door activation button. The door hissed. It lowered.

It was getting very dark outside.

Braddox didn't wait for the door to open fully before climbing into the ship. "Shut the door!"

"Founding!" Candice wore a huge smile. She held her arms out, open wide.

"You made it," he said, dropping to his knees and pulling her into his arms. "I knew you would. I knew you'd get back to the ship."

"Are you okay?"

"I am. I'm good."

"You have to weld her leg closed," Aria said, anxious to delegate the assignment.

They ignored her.

"A meteor shower is headed this way."

"How long?" Braddox said.

"Not positive, but we have to get off this planet. Now."

"Where's Caldera?"

"Didn't make it," Candice said. "It's the three of us."

"Okay." Braddox stood up. He grabbed the welder and Candice's blaster.

"What are you doing?" Aria said.

"The fuel tank's not repaired. I need to finish that up. We aren't going anywhere with a hole in the tank. It was nearly done. This won't take long," he said, and smiled.

He was lying.

"Can I help?"

"We're going to fix her leg. That needs to be done first."

"Fix it, not weld it?" Aria said.

"No. We're welding it. That will cauterize everything and sterilize it as well. We have no idea what type of bacteria is out there, what we're actually breathing in."

"Thanks," Candice said. It was half-hearted sarcasm.

"I have air samples," Aria said.

"Analyse it later. Right now, I need your help."

Braddox worked fast. He drew his knife along the leg of the suit up to Candice's groin and then pulled the fabric apart. It didn't tear easily. He kept chopping at it with the blade until her entire thigh was exposed. "We need water," he said, "and something for her to bite down on."

Aria ran to the small fridge. She removed a bottle of water and found a wood spoon in the cupboard. "Here," she said.

Braddox opened the water and doused it over the stump. He used his hand and wiped away dry blood. Then, he placed a welders shield on he his head, but hadn't lowered the mask.

Aria closed her mouth hard. She didn't want to vomit. She felt bile speed up her throat. Swallowing it down took some doing.

"Get behind her," Braddox said. "Put her head in your lap, and the spoon in her mouth. You're going to have to hold her down. Press on her shoulders. Understand me? She can't move. She's going to fight you, but it's your job to keep her still."

Aria lifted Candice's head and set it on her lap. She tried putting the spoon in Candice's mouth as if feeding her soup.

Braddox took the spoon out of Aria's hand, shaking his head, and placed it long ways, the handle in Candice's mouth. "Bite down on that," he said.

Candice's forehead was sweating. Her eyes were wide. The woman knew what was about to happen would hurt. She was talking, despite the spoon. "Do it quick, man. Quick."

"I will," Braddox said, and then nodded up at Aria.

Aria leaned over Candice's head and pressed down on her shoulders, her hands clasped on Candice's arms.

"I mean hold her down good, you got me?" Braddox said.

Aria nodded.

"Don't look at the arc," he said, lowering the mask. "Either of you."

Aria shut her eyes. She had no intention of watching the surgery anyway. She didn't need to be instructed otherwise.

She heard the welding gun spark to life.

Even with her eyes closed, the bright white and blue light pierced her eyelids.

Candice bucked. Her body writhed. She released a muffled screamed, tongue pressed against the wood spoon in her mouth.

The pungent odor of burning flesh filled Aria's nostrils. She again worried she was going to throw up. Her stomach lurched and rolled. She was able to hold it down. For now.

Candice thrashed. Her hips twisted. Aria opened one eye, doing her best not to look at the arc.

"Hold still," Braddox said. He pressed one hand down on her thigh just above the stump. Smoke rose off the severed ends of torn meat and skin. "Done. I'm done."

Aria looked down at Candice.

Her eyes were closed.

"She passed out," Braddox said. "Keep an eye on her. I'm going out to finish the repairs on the fuel tank."

"I don't think that's a good idea. It's night time. There are going to be more predators out there." Aria didn't want to be left alone.

"If I don't do this, we don't get off this planet."

Aria didn't say anything. She couldn't argue with that.

"I'll be quick. There wasn't much left," he said. "If anything happens, by my chair is a switch that says autopilot—"

"I know about the autopilot," she said.

"It will start the engines, take off, and fly you right back to Clandestine. You won't have to do a thing," he said, collecting up the gear he wanted for finishing the job.

"Then why don't we just leave now. Fix the tank later."

Braddox stopped what he was doing. "Truth is, if you take off before that tank's fixed, there's a fifty-fifty chance you'll make it back to Clandestine. Fifty-fifty is generous. I need to rig the odds in our favor. We spilled fuel on the way down. The gage wasn't reading properly. I have no idea how much we lost. That kills the odds, cutting them in half right there. Let me do this, okay? It won't take long."

It was the first time Aria felt he was honest with her. He didn't sugarcoat the situation. She had only been fooling herself anyway. They were in trouble. She didn't need an explanation from him. She knew it. His confirmation just made everything more real. "Be quick," she said.

He grabbed a new helmet off a hook by the door.

"Kind of late for that now, don't you think?"

He put it on. He pressed the comm link on the shoulder of his suit. "Test, one, two. Test."

His voice came out from speakers on the bridge.

"This way we can keep in contact," he said.

She smiled. "Good thinking."

He opened the shuttle door. He checked left and right before exiting the ship.

She closed the door and tended to Candice. She used a wet cloth over her forehead and face, washing away stale perspiration and blood.

Inside the ship, she heard Braddox working. She wished it was quieter repairs. The noise would attract more giant lizards, predatory birds, dangerous rodents, and whatever else was out there that she'd not yet seen.

She cried.

There was no sense holding it in. Not anymore. Candice was still out of it, and she was alone.

Even though her father was dead, he was the one person she wanted to see most when she arrived back home. He would have been so proud of her. He'd be standing by the platform waiting for her to exit Clandestine. She'd run to him, jump in his arms, and he'd lift her off her feet and spin her around welcoming her back as his hero.

No one would be waiting for her if she ever made it home.

She had no family, no close friends.

There was no one.

Whether home or here, she was alone.

CHAPTER 17

Aria sat in the co-pilot seat. She stared out at the terrain. The tall trees had wonderful large green leaves. The thick grass blades were long, and thick, and sharp. The planet had one moon. She'd not noticed it when they landed. It was out now and sat like a soft white ball amid the starlit sky. The moon's glow reached the surface and provided reflective light from the solar system's main star.

It was a beautiful planet. She wished there'd been time to explore the mountains and caves she'd seen. Aside from crazy monsters that would try eating them, she bet the place was a wonder begging for exploration. Although the air was breathable, Braddox's concern about foreign bacteria was something she should have thought of first. Who knew what festered inside of them. Alien *beings* she would hopefully shed during decontamination once back on *Clandestine*.

She didn't want to dwell on it. The idea of foreign germs infecting her was frightening.

"Light?"

Braddox was on the intercom. She grabbed the headset and held the mic near her mouth. "This is Light."

"I am finishing up. I think we're in good shape. Over."

That was the first good thing she'd heard all day. "Roger."

"I've just got to finish up one thing, and we can say goodbye to this place forever. Over."

"Music to my ears, captain. Out."

She set down the headset and smiled. It didn't seem possible. Part of her expected more to go wrong. It was more than a pessimistic outlook. It was more of an impending feeling of complete doom. Her mind often got the best of her. Her imagination ran wild. She'd mastered keeping those feelings to herself. Without control of her emotions, she'd never have been selected for the mission, would never have passed the psychological evaluations. It wasn't that she cheated on the tests and during the interviews as much as she twisted words and answers accordingly to accommodate what was needed in order to pass.

"Light? Go to autopilot. Now!"

Aria stood up. She placed palms on the dash. Out in front of the ship, Braddox ran toward the jungle.

"Light!" Braddox said.

"Help me over there," Candice said.

Aria ran over and lifted Candice, getting under one arm. "Lean on me," she said.

"Put me in Founding's chair," she said.

Aria and Candice hobbled forward. Aria couldn't take her eyes off the front shield. One of the large spiked spine lizards was after him.

Candice sat in the pilot's chair. She flipped switches and pressed buttons. Lights came on, and engines started.

The spine spiked lizard stopped, rose up tall, and roared. Maybe Braddox was no longer as interesting as a spaceship.

"Get that thing out of here," Braddox said over the comm.

"Roger," Candice said.

"You flying?"

"Roger, again," Candice said. She lowered the mic. "Go to the arsenal. Grab the Laser-blast."

"And do what with it?" Aria said.

"Go!"

Liberation lifted off the ground.

Braddox was outside waving his arms, trying to draw the lizard's attention.

"Aria!"

"Coming!"

"Open the side door. Stand on the landing."

"Stand on the landing?"

"And kill that thing!" Candice said.

Braddox ran at the lizard. He was trying desperately to save them.

Aria palmed the button. The door hissed as it opened slowly and then lowered. The stairs led nowhere unless she wanted to jump twenty feet. She stood in the jamb, the gun strap slung over her shoulder, and readied the weapon, taking it off stun.

Liberation had to be twenty feet in the air.

She was eye level to the spiked spine lizard. It opened its mouth and roared. Saliva shot off its tongue and sharp teeth and sprayed into the ship. Coated in lizard drool, Aria turned the weapon on the creature and fired.

A red blast rocketed out of the muzzle. The laser cut a burn across the side of the monster's face below the eye and above the jaw.

It lifted its head and roared again, only this time it sounded higher pitched, as if screaming.

It brought its head down; the front of its long snout whacked the bottom of the door. The ship twisted in air. Aria stumbled back a step, before falling forward. She dropped out of Liberation. The weapon strap was lodged on the corner of the door, the snaps on the weapon bending from her weight.

Aria refused to look down or behind her. She reached up with her free hand. Her fingers were inches away from the bottom of the door. Falling was not an option. If she didn't do something fast, it wouldn't matter. The spiked spine lizard would eat her. Simple as that.

Candice must have been fighting with the controls. She regained balance and the ship continued to climb into the air.

Unable to stop, Aria looked down.

The lizard jumped, jaws snapping. Its snout was close to taking off her legs.

The blaster strap was going to snap. The fall would kill her, she hoped. Death from dropping out of the ship would be better than getting torn apart by the lizard.

The ship tilted to the right. Aria's body slammed against the door. She moved quickly, planting her feet against the hull and climbing upward. Her hand latched onto the opened door, and she pulled herself up. It wasn't easy. She was physically drained. A little at a time. Her arms felt like rubber, as if there were no muscle tone at all. There was no quitting. Candice had given her a second chance. She had to make it back inside the ship.

It was a last effort attempt. She grunted and groaned and pulled. She was up and halfway in. She repositioned her hands and pushed and dragged herself inside.

The blaster fell away.

She threw herself into the ship. "I'm in," she said. "I'm in!"

"Braddox is still down there," Candice said.

Aria stood up, retrieved another blaster, and went back to the open door. "Get me just a little closer."

Candice lowered the ship.

Aria could see the top of the lizard's head. "That's good. Hold it steady."

"Doing my best," she said.

Aria ventured out onto the open door, again. She held the blaster with both hands and took aim. Her shots struck the lizard's skull. It looked up at *Liberation*, roaring continuously. Its small arms with tiny hands waved around as if trying to reach the ship.

She thought about Martin while she fired shots at the animal.

The mission wasn't to interfere. It was to observe and gather samples.

It sounded good on paper and when it was explained during briefings.

She didn't take her finger off the trigger.

The lizard stumbled back and finally went down. The sound of its body crashing on the ground was thunderous. "Get me closer," Aria said.

"It's dead."

"It is not. It's still moving. Closer!" Aria watched her shots slam into the softer side of the thing's belly. The burning holes smoked.

Its eyes remained open. They stared at Aria.

She fired more shots into the lizard's gut. She had no intention of stopping until the blaster ran out of ammunition, or the lizard combusted bursting into flames.

"We're landing," Candice said. "Back inside."

Aria let off three more rounds and then reluctantly stepped back into the ship. Braddox Founding ran toward the door. He was close.

She imagined a lizard taking him down just before he reached the ship.

The image flashed across her mind over and over with every step he took.

She couldn't risk that happening. She jumped out of Liberation and aimed the blaster left and right and left, there was nothing.

Braddox grabbed her arm as he ran past her, pulling her with him back onto the ship. "Doppler, get us out of here!"

"Aye, captain."

Thrusters flared.

Braddox hit the button to close the door.

"Hold onto something," Candice said.

The ship shot into the sky.

CHAPTER 18

Aria buckled in behind Candice in the jump seat. Braddox sat in the co-pilot chair.

"Fuel gage," he said, tapping a glass plated instrument on the panel. "We've got three quarters remaining. Should be plenty to reach—"

Aria looked up when the captain stopped talking.

Liberation was on its way up toward space.

Balls on fire sped toward them, flaming tails trailing behind.

"Captain?" Candice said.

"You can do this," Braddox said. "Two rules. Simple rules. One, don't hit one of the meteors."

"And the second rule?" Aria said.

Candice and Braddox said the second rule together: "Don't get hit by one of the meteors."

They laughed.

Aria had no idea what was so funny. She latched onto the armrests in white knuckle grips. She didn't even blink watching the shower rain down around them.

Candice handled *Liberation* well, though.

They zigged. They zagged. Meteors flew by the ship far too close. The worse part were the sounds of explosions on the planet below them.

"We need to get out of this atmosphere fast," Braddox said.

"Working on it," Candice said.

"Aftershock has got to be rippling across everything below us," he said.

# # #

They were in space, away from the clutches of the shower. As they made their way back to *Clandestine*, they watched in awe and horror as the planet was pummeled by meteors. The mass grouping of chunky rocks tumbled directly toward the planet.

"That one," Braddox said. He didn't need to point. They all saw it.

In the center of the shower, and speeding faster than the other rocks at the already damaged planet, was a massive sized meteor. It pierced the atmosphere and looked as if it immediately caught on fire. The tail of flames zipped along behind it.

"I almost can't watch," Aria said. She didn't close her eyes. She couldn't look away.

It took seconds before the meteor slammed into water. The high velocity impact was visible in space. The halo blast rippled around where it crashed and spread out over the sea and onto land. It looked as if most of the planet was going to cave in on itself, as if the meteor had bore a hole through the crust and everything would be sucked down to the core. Aria fully expected the entire world to explode from the inside out.

"Azure?" Braddox said. He shook his head.

"What?" Aria said.

"Did I hear you tell Caldera if you could name the planet, you would call it Azure?" he said.

"Yeah. That was before we landed."

"That means blue, right? It's a shade?"

Aria nodded. "It is."

"I don't think a single one of those lizards is going to survive this space shower. It'll be questionable if the world doesn't collapse soon. Look at how many meteors are still headed right for them. I've got a better name for that forsaken place, though," he said.

"And what is that?"

"Obsidian," he said. "It means—"

"I know what it means," Aria said. "I think Obsidian is a much more appropriate name."

CHAPTER 19

Captain Braddox Founding let Candice Doppler land *Liberation* inside *Clandestine's* bay.

The decontamination showers lasted nearly an hour long. The spray was meant to enter their pores and to be breathed in. It worked as it raced through their systems. Hot water was mixed with special suds. Rough bristles scrub their skin raw.

Aria didn't complain; she worried mostly about Candice. Machine Techs didn't know to be careful with her stump. Aria heard her scream a few times. She could only imagine how bad it hurt when the bristles scraped over the wound.

Dressed in fresh clothing, they met back at *Liberation* where they transferred the sleep pods back onto *Clandestine*.

"We'll get these refreshed, resupplied, make our vlog reports, send them home ahead of us, and then it will be beddy-bye time," Braddox said.

"But I'm not tired," Candice said.

It wasn't funny. Aria didn't want to sleep. She had already been asleep for ten years. They'd only just woken up a day ago. One day. And now he wanted them all just to go back to sleep for ten more years?

"We do have one option," Braddox said. "It goes against protocol."

"And we can stay up a while?" Aria said, knowing she sounded far too eager. She didn't care. She was more stimulated now than she had been leaving home to reach. . .Obsidian.

"Doppler's in a bad way," Braddox said.

"Such a way with words," Candice said.

"Well, I'm just being serious. We can rig the pod to feed her meds and antibiotics, but that dressing is going to need changing two or three times a day for the next few weeks. That wound is going to need some air, too. We need to keep an eye on it for infection. Can't do any of those things if we're asleep," Braddox said. "Aside from Candice, we don't all have to stay awake. . ."

"I'm in," Aria said. "She's going to need help. She can't do everything on her own."

Braddox smiled. "I propose we hit the pods in a month, maybe six weeks, after we see how she's healing. How's that sound?"

"Like a plan," Aria said.

The sleep pods were connected to slow-feed and hydration intake tubes as well as waste outtake hoses. The setup process was simple enough. Gages were calibrated and power supply sources verified, as well as the back-up power supply, and the back-up to the back-up power supply.

Aria brushed her hands on her pants and made her way up toward Clandestine's bridge.

Clandestine was six times as large as Liberation. Batteries and power sources, combined with tracking and computer mapping systems, made up most of the electrical aspects of the ship. There were two levels, and a third was dedicated to engines and light speed.

Engineers at home used keypads and joysticks that remote controlled the entire ship. Animatronics and robot-like technicians ambled about the halls handling repairs, as well as taking care of circuit boards, and other electrical issues behind the scene. Software upgrades and patches were done from home as well. So when Captain Braddox went to sleep with the rest of the crew and turned over leadership, it was as if an invisible crew took over at the helm.

"Obsidian," Aria said.

"What was that?" Candice said. She hobbled up next to her using a crutch to support her weight.

"Nothing," Aria said. "Should you be up and about like this?"

"I'm getting in a little bit of exercise in before sleep," she said. "I just finished recording my vlog. I'm headed to my chamber. I may not be ready for a ten year sleep, but right now, I could stand an eight hour nap."

Aria placed a hand on her shoulder. They looked at each other for a moment. The silence between them was filled with mutual understanding.

"I'll be up shortly," Aria said. "I'm beat, too."

Candice Doppler nodded and carefully walked away.

# # #

"Light, could you report to the bridge?" Braddox's voice resounded over the P.A. system.

Aria made her way through the halls and onto the bridge. "Captain?"

"Caldera had items in his bag," he said. "Did you see what he'd collected?"

"Some rock samples. Dirt. Some other things as well. I'm not positive. His bag was down in Liberation."

"I retrieved his bag and yours. I was going to catalogue items," Braddox said.

"I could do that, Captain. Now that we have some extra time to get things done."

"Well, the thing is, I dropped his bag on the way up."

"And?"

"*And* have a look at this." On the table, the bag unzipped, were three large rocks.

Aria remembered seeing Martin stuff the rocks into his bag. "What about them?"

He pointed to the rock in the center. "Rocks don't crack," he said.

They both gathered around the rocks and bent forward, getting close.

"It's not a rock," Aria said, stating the obvious.

"It's an egg."

Her breath caught in her lungs. "We should flush it out, captain, get it off the ship!"

The crack was narrow, starting at the rounded top of the egg and extending out in a few different directions.

"That was my first thought, Light," he said. He finger tapped the base of the egg.

It rocked back and forth a little. It didn't move from the tap. It wiggled because of it.

"Captain, we can't fly back home with those lizards on board," she said.

"I've got a thought," he said.

She shook her head.

"You haven't even heard it yet," he said.

"You can tell me, but it's not going to change my mind."

"Just listen, what if we stick the unhatched eggs in a cryogenics chamber. If the specimen don't make it, our lab boys home can bisect and dissect the creatures until they have answers to whatever questions they think of," he said.

"And if they don't die?"

"Same thing," he said.

"And what about this one?" She pointed to the cracked egg.

Small finger-link limbs poked out of the shell. The green lizard hand pulled and pushed at a section until it fell free from the rest of the egg.

"This one we stick in Caldera's sleep pod and it will barely age. We alter the food and water, and in ten years. . ."

"That's not right. We shouldn't do that," Aria said.

"You think we should kill it?" Braddox said.

"We should flush all of them out. Launch them into space," Aria said.

"You could do that?"

The lizard's head poked out next.

She couldn't be certain. She thought it was a baby spiked spine lizard. A spinosaurus, if she were given the chance to name it. It cawed like a bird, snout open.

"If you want to do it, it's your call. I won't stop you," he said.

Aria stood up straight. She set fisted hands on her hips. All at once she grabbed up the bag with the eggs. She marched off the bridge. Braddox wasn't following behind her. She went to the nearest bathroom and opened the door. Setting the bag down in the sink she lifted the toilet lid.

"You have no right coming home with us. Our planet doesn't need more problems," she said.

The lizard was mostly out of the egg. Its body was covered in a thin, grey yolk. Its tongue lapped at yolk, cleaning itself off. Its eyelids closed and opened. The thing was looking right at her.

She didn't believe in imprinting.

Okay. She believed in it, knew it happened with many types of animals. She didn't care though. That was the difference.

She scooped the lizard into cupped hands and held him over the bowl.

Lifting a leg, she used her toe to flush the toilet.

There was no water like at home. Just suction.

The suction was so intense they were taught not to be sitting when they engaged the flush feature. The suction was so powerful she wondered if it helped power the ship.

The flush ended.

She looked down.

The lizard was still in her hands.

She shook her head at the creature. "No," she said. "Uh-uh."

It had crawled around on her palm, tiny hands wrapped around her thumb. Its mouth closed over her knuckle. It gnawed at her skin. Tiny teeth bit into her, but weren't large enough to cut through flesh.

She kicked out with her leg, and she flushed the toilet a second time.

# # #

The cryogenics chamber spilled out steam until the sliding door sealed shut. The unhatched eggs were frozen in a matter of seconds. Those eggs wouldn't hatch—shouldn't hatch—until thawed.

"He seems to like you," Braddox said.

They walked to Martin's sleep pod. Braddox had moved it to a secure part of the ship. The area was made of reinforced steel, meant for hiding or storing valuable cargo.

"Spinosaurus? I like it. You're good with naming things," Braddox said.

"Except that planet," Aria said.

"If everything down there didn't try to eat us, and the meteor shower didn't destroy almost the entire planet, Azure would have been perfect," he said.

The sleep pod slid open.

Aria placed the lizard inside. "He won't grow while he's in there?"

"Shouldn't. Maybe a little," Braddox said.

"And you think this is the right thing, bringing a living, breathing creature like this home?"

"We've got video and audio of just about everything that happened back there. I think after they see the footage, they're going to be very curious about getting their hands on this little guy," he said.

She hated that he made it sound like a cute, harmless pet.

It wasn't.

It wouldn't be, anyway.

"You're the captain," she said.

The lizard leapt in the air, trying to get back in her hands.

Braddox closed the sleep pod lid. He activated the sleeping gas.

It took less than twenty seconds before the baby lizard was out cold.

EPILOGUE

"My name is Aria Light. I was one of two scientists on board Clandestine. Martin Caldera died courageously saving my life. If it weren't for him, I would not be here right now.

"Our mission was simple: Find a suitable planet for colonization. At this time, Obsidian is dangerous. That's what we've decided to call it. The Black Planet. Obsidian.

"Carnivorous lifeforms was half of the problem. The meteor shower we witnessed was the other half. If any species survived the storm, I'd be surprised.

"I would not rule out this planet, though. It has potential. The air is breathable. There is plenty of water, and the ground appears fertile for growing food. I have collected samples I will be testing as soon as we're home."

Home.

She suddenly missed Obsidian. What was it that made returning home worth while?

The planet was dying, perhaps in worse shape and sicker than the one they'd just fled.

The lizards on Obsidian might all be dead now.

Her planet was nearly extinct. . .

About the Author

Phillip Tomasso is the author of over 17 novels, and over one hundred short stories. He works full time as a Fire / EMS Dispatcher for 911. His three children are what is most important in his life. In his spare time he plays guitar, and is always at work on his next novel.

www.philliptomasso.com
Email: phillip@philliptomasso.com
Twitter: @P_Tomasso

Special Thanks

As indicated in the dedication, I want to thank my daughter. Severed Press was looking for Dino stories. I racked my brain for ideas. My daughter just turned and looked at me and said, "Hey, dad? What if. . ." I want to thank all of my beta readers, but especially Karen Dziegiel, for reading through drafts and responding with comments and suggestions quickly. Input like that in invaluable. I would like to extend a most gracious Thank You to my proofreader, and dear friend, Linda Tooch. And, as always, I want to thank Gary Lucas, and his staff at Severed Press.

Other Novels

MIND PLAY
TENTH HOUSE
THIRD RING
JOHNNY BLADE
ADVERSE IMPACT
THE MOLECH PROPHECY (writing as Thomas Phillips)
PULSE OF EVIL
CONVICTED
PIGEON DROP
SOUNDS OF SILENCE
VACCINATION
EVACUATION
PRESERVATION
TREASURE ISLAND: A Zombie Novella
BLOOD RIVER
DAMN THE DEAD
YOUNG BLOOD: The Nightbreed Saga (co-written with Phil Tomasso IV)

www.ingramcontent.com/pod-product-compliance
Lightning Source LLC
Chambersburg PA
CBHW030555130626
46552CB00006B/2556